CIVIC VIRTUE
LET'S WORK TOGETHER

HOW RULES AND LAWS CHANGE SOCIETY

JOSHUA TURNER

PowerKiDS press

New York

Published in 2019 by The Rosen Publishing Group, Inc.
29 East 21st Street, New York, NY 10010

First Edition

Editor: Melissa Raé Shofner
Book Design: Tanya Dellaccio

Photo Credits: Cover GordonsLife/E+/Getty Images; p. 4 vichie81/Shutterstock.com; p. 5 Elena Nichizhenova/Shutterstock.com; p. 7 Steven Frame/Shutterstock.com; p. 8 Taren Cassidy/EyeEm/Getty Images; p. 9 Sergey Novikov/Shutterstock.com; p. 11 (Congress meeting) https://commons.wikimedia.org/wiki/File:Obama_Health_Care_Speech_to_Joint_Session_of_Congress.jpg; p. 11 (Capitol Building) Orhan Cam/Shutterstock.com; p. 13 SewCream/Shutterstock.com; p. 15 (boys playing chess) Mladen Mitrinovic/Shutterstock.com; p. 15 (girls with sign) Robert Kneschke/Shutterstock.com; p. 17 https://commons.wikimedia.org/wiki/File:Scene_at_the_Signing_of_the_Constitution_of_the_United_States.jpg; p. 19 (classroom in China) jianbing Lee/Shutterstock.com; p. 19 (classroom in South Africa) Gimas/Shutterstock.com; p. 21 (United Nations Assembly Hall) Marco Brivio/Photographer's Choice/Getty Images; p. 21 (United Nations Building) S. Greg Panosian/E+/Getty Images; p. 22 michaeljung/Shutterstock.com.

Cataloging-in-Publication Data

Names: Turner, Joshua.
Title: How rules and laws change society / Joshua Turner.
Description: New York : PowerKids Press, 2019. | Series: Civic virtue: let's work together | Includes index.
Identifiers: LCCN ISBN 9781508166771 (pbk.) | ISBN 9781508166757 (library bound) | ISBN 9781508166788 (6 pack)
Subjects: LCSH: Law–Juvenile literature. | Social norms–Juvenile literature.
Classification: LCC K246.T87 2019 | DDC 340'.1–dc23

Manufactured in the United States of America

CPSIA Compliance Information: Batch #CS18PK: For Further Information contact Rosen Publishing, New York, New York at 1-800-237-9932

CONTENTS

SOCIETIES NEED RULES

A society is a group of people that have common values, morals, and ideas. In order for a society to work properly, it must have rules and laws that people in the society follow.

Think of your classroom as an example of a small society. You and your fellow students all want the same thing: to learn and have fun doing it! But in order for society—and your classroom—to be successful, there must be rules.

THE WHITE HOUSE

THINK ABOUT WHAT IT MIGHT BE LIKE IF THERE WEREN'T ANY RULES IN YOUR CLASSROOM. WOULD YOU STILL BE ABLE TO LEARN?

CITIZENS IN ACTION

IN THE UNITED STATES, THE GOVERNMENT DECIDES RULES AND LAWS. THERE ARE GOVERNMENTS AT THE LOCAL, STATE, AND NATIONAL LEVELS.

RULES AND LAWS

Rules and laws make it so everyone in a society is treated fairly. They also make it so everyone has the same rights and **responsibilities**. In order for rules and laws to be fair, they must be the same for everyone. When specific individuals are treated differently, rules and laws become useless.

Rules and laws can be big and small but they're all important. They tell us how we're supposed to act at any given place or time.

THE U.S. SUPREME COURT IS LOCATED IN WASHINGTON, D.C. IT'S THE MOST IMPORTANT COURT IN THE UNITED STATES. ▶

TEAMWORK GETS THINGS DONE

Why do people live in a society at all? Part of the reason is because people can do great things when they work together as a team.

Think of your favorite team sport. Imagine how much harder and less fun it would be if, instead of working as a team, it was every person for themselves. Teammates help each other out and do what's best for the team. In the same way, citizens in a society work together, too.

SOME ANIMALS HAVE SOCIETIES, TOO. IN THE WILD, LIONS LIVE IN SOCIAL GROUPS CALLED PRIDES. LIFE WOULD BE HARDER FOR THEM ALONE. LIONS HAVE RULES, SUCH AS AN EATING ORDER, THAT MUST BE FOLLOWED TO STAY IN THEIR PRIDE.

WHO MAKES RULES AND LAWS?

In the United States, local, state, and national governments make rules and laws. People in society elect officials to run these governments.

The elected officials are **representatives** for society. They're trusted to make laws and rules that are fair and just. If they don't, they may be **replaced** in an election. In a classroom, the teacher makes the rules. This is because the teacher is believed to be the best judge of what is fair for everyone in the class.

THE U.S. CAPITOL BUILDING IS WHERE THE HOUSE OF REPRESENTATIVES AND THE SENATE MEET. IT'S WHERE ELECTED CONGRESSPEOPLE GO TO **DEBATE** AND VOTE ON LAWS.

CONGRESS MEETING

CITIZENS IN ACTION

IN THE UNITED STATES, CITIZENS VOTE FOR A PRESIDENT EVERY 4 YEARS, SENATORS EVERY 6 YEARS, AND CONGRESSPEOPLE EVERY 2 YEARS. THIS MEANS ELECTED OFFICIALS MUST MAKE RULES AND LAWS THAT THE MAJORITY OF PEOPLE LIKE, OR THEY MAY NOT BE REELECTED.

U.S. CAPITOL BUILDING

LIFE WITHOUT RULES

If there were no rules or laws, there could be no society. Rules and laws help people understand what their **obligations** are to society and to others in it.

Imagine your own classroom without rules. How would you be able to learn or go to lunch or have recess? Imagine trying to play a game with no rules. It wouldn't be much fun. While rules may sometimes seem bothersome, they're necessary to be able to play the game.

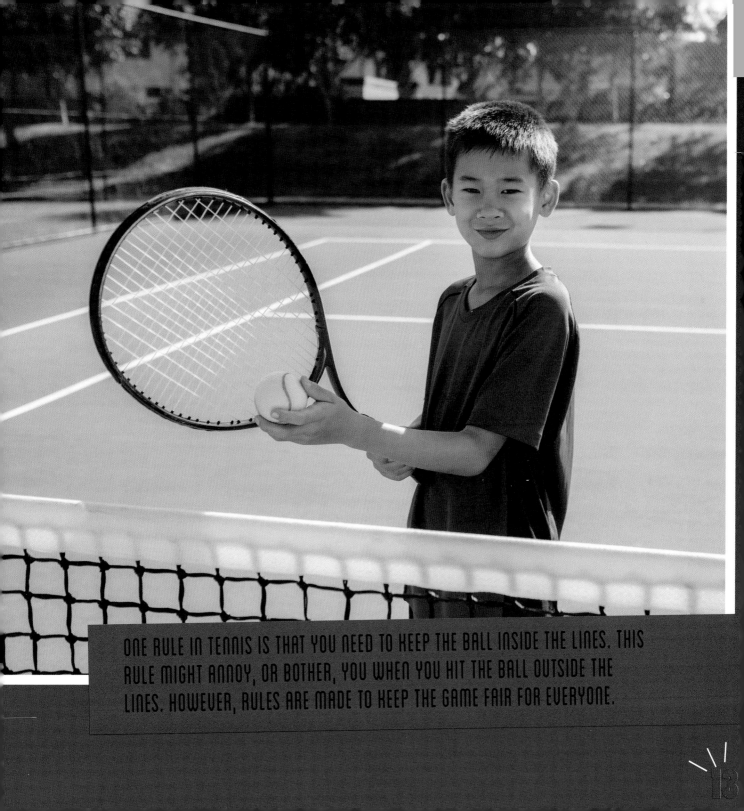

ONE RULE IN TENNIS IS THAT YOU NEED TO KEEP THE BALL INSIDE THE LINES. THIS RULE MIGHT ANNOY, OR BOTHER, YOU WHEN YOU HIT THE BALL OUTSIDE THE LINES. HOWEVER, RULES ARE MADE TO KEEP THE GAME FAIR FOR EVERYONE.

13

TOO MANY RULES!

Having too many rules can be almost as bad as having no rules at all. If a society has too many rules, people may become angry or annoyed. This might also happen if a society has rules that don't make sense or rules that aren't needed.

Imagine having so many rules at home all you could do was sit in your bedroom. You probably wouldn't be very happy. Too many rules could change society in a bad way.

SOMETIMES BOARD GAMES HAVE SO MANY RULES THEY AREN'T FUN. HAVING TOO MANY RULES LIMITS CREATIVITY AND IMAGINATION, WHICH CAN MAKE THINGS SEEM TEDIOUS, OR BORING.

CITIZENS IN ACTION

PEOPLE MIGHT **PROTEST** IF THEY FEEL THERE ARE TOO MANY LAWS OR THAT CERTAIN LAWS ARE UNFAIR. PROTESTS ARE A WAY OF LETTING LAWMAKERS KNOW WHAT THEY'RE DOING WRONG AND CAN MAKE CHANGE MORE LIKELY.

DIFFERENT SOCIETIES, DIFFERENT RULES

In the United States, the most important rules and laws are found in the **Constitution**. Freedom of speech, freedom of **religion**, and the right to a fair **trial** are just some of the rules found in this document.

Societies around the world have different rules and laws. This is because not all people can agree on what rules and laws are important. Each society is different from the others, sometimes in big ways and sometimes in small ways.

AT THE CONSTITUTIONAL CONVENTION, THE FIRST REPRESENTATIVES OF THE UNITED STATES DEBATED OVER WHAT THE RULES OF THEIR NEW SOCIETY SHOULD BE. THESE ARE THE SAME RULES AND LAWS WE LIVE BY TODAY.

THE **AMERICAN REVOLUTION** CAME ABOUT BECAUSE THE **COLONISTS** DIDN'T LIKE LIVING UNDER GREAT BRITAIN'S RULES. YEARS OF PROTESTS FINALLY LED THE COLONISTS TO BREAK AWAY TO FORM THEIR OWN SOCIETY AND CREATE THEIR OWN LAWS.

THE INTERNATIONAL SOCIETY

We know the United States is a society, but what about other countries? There are many countries in the world. Each of them helps make up the **international** society.

Think of your class at school. It's just one in a whole building full of classrooms. They all have some features that are alike but each one is different in important ways. There are also many other schools, which are also full of classrooms. Altogether, these schools make up a society of schools.

CLASSROOM, SOUTH AFRICA

ALL THE COUNTRIES ON EARTH HAVE DIFFERENT SOCIETIES, AND EACH HAS DIFFERENT RULES AND LAWS. THIS IS PART OF WHAT MAKES EACH COUNTRY SPECIAL.

CLASSROOM, CHINA

INTERNATIONAL LAWS AND RULES

Just like you should want to get along with students from other classrooms, countries around the world should also want to get along with each other. This means there needs to be some rules and laws for countries to follow.

Without general rules and laws, countries may go to war to settle their differences. Having agreed-upon laws helps countries avoid disagreements and fights. It may also change the way countries interact, or deal with each other.

THE UNITED NATIONS IS WHERE INTERNATIONAL LEADERS MEET TO TALK ABOUT THE RULES AND LAWS THEIR COUNTRIES FOLLOW. THIS IS SIMILAR TO HOW LAWS ARE MADE IN A SOCIETY. COUNTRIES, HOWEVER, AGREE TO FOLLOW RULES AND LAWS IN GOOD FAITH RATHER THAN BECAUSE OF FEAR OF GETTING IN TROUBLE.

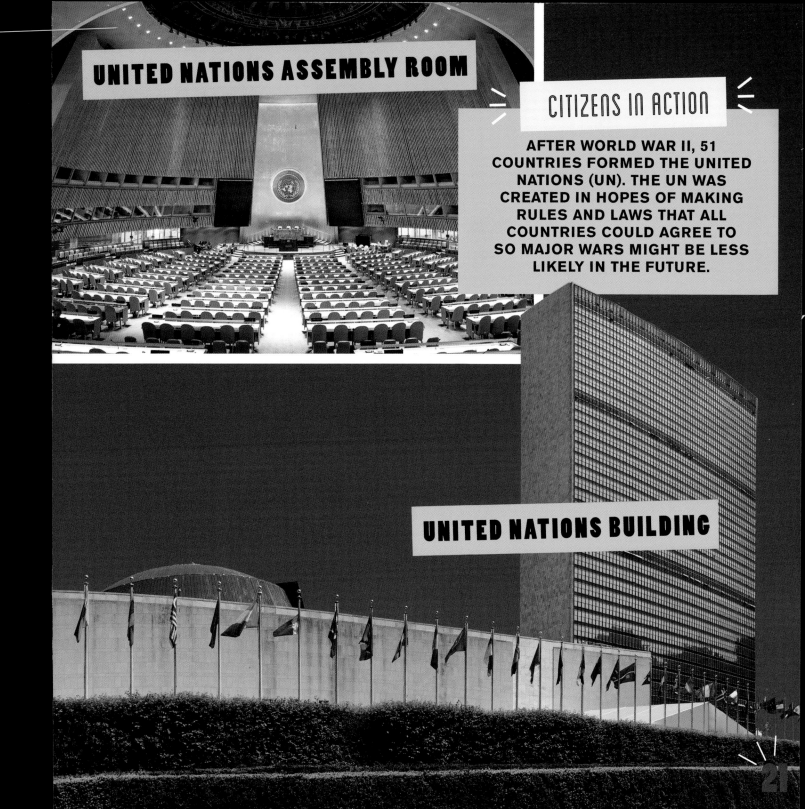

UNITED NATIONS ASSEMBLY ROOM

CITIZENS IN ACTION

AFTER WORLD WAR II, 51 COUNTRIES FORMED THE UNITED NATIONS (UN). THE UN WAS CREATED IN HOPES OF MAKING RULES AND LAWS THAT ALL COUNTRIES COULD AGREE TO SO MAJOR WARS MIGHT BE LESS LIKELY IN THE FUTURE.

UNITED NATIONS BUILDING

CHANGING SOCIETY

Societies are shaped by the laws and rules people agree to. If there are no rules or laws, there can be no societies. If there are no societies, people's lives would be worse.

Rules and laws—whether they are made by the government, a teacher, or a parent—are important. They help us live our daily lives in peaceful and meaningful ways. Rules and laws change societies, and they show what the people in each society think is most important.

GLOSSARY

American Revolution: A war that lasted from 1775 to 1783 in which the American colonists won independence from British rule.

colonist: Someone who lives in a colony, which is a piece of land under the control of another country.

Constitution: The writing that lists the basic laws of the United States.

debate: To argue a side.

international: Involving two or more countries.

obligation: Something someone has to do.

protest: To object to an idea, an act, or a way of doing something.

religion: A belief in and way of honoring a god or gods.

replace: To take the place of something else.

representative: One who stands for a group of people; a member of a lawmaking body who acts for voters.

responsibility: Something a person is in charge of.

trial: When a case is decided in a court of law.

INDEX

WEBSITES

Due to the changing nature of Internet links, PowerKids Press has developed an
online list of websites related to the subject of this book. This site is updated regularly.
Please use this link to access the list: www.powerkidslinks.com/civicv/rlsoc